BORN OF
THE SEA

The Untold Story of Anne Bonny

and Mary Read

- A NOVELLA -

KATE CASTLE

Published by Dark Horse Publishing LLP

www.darkhorsepublishing.co.uk

ISBN: 978-1-9169031-1-1

First Edition Printed: May 2021

Cover design by Mary O'Brien.

* Cover quotes taken from ARC reader reviews.

Front cover illustration copyright Yuliya Derbisheva

© 123RF.com

Back cover illustration copyright Tetiana Syrytsyna

© 123RF.com

DARK HORSE PUBLISHING

For Tim, Lucy, Rory and Alice.

My crewmates.

3

'The real voyage of discovery consists not in seeking new landscapes, but in having new eyes.'

- Marcel Proust

1

My name, in those days, was Anne Bonny. I'm told I was born in Cork, Ireland, sometime before 1700, but my father never told me the year, nor the day nor month of my birth. I should think he never really cared enough to know. Later, I would imagine I was born at sea in a night tempest; mountainous waves throwing the ship around like a twig in a rolling barrel of grog, my mother spread-eagled on the deck, her hair splayed out, screaming like a wild banshee. The sea has always felt like my true birthplace. It is where I found myself. It is where I found Mary.

I regret that neither my birth nor my early life was quite that romantic, however. I was an illegitimate child of my father – a lawyer – and his housemaid. To escape the scandal, and his wife's wrath, my father dressed me as a boy and passed me off as a young clerk, opening legal letters and such. That was until my chest started to grow in, and my rosy cheeks and lips likened to those of a lady. Gentlemen and not-so-gentle-men began to pay me attention. Whether or not they knew I was a lass I do not know, but they nevertheless took a liking to me, be it a boy or girl they were after. More than once, I had to fight a fellow off, which was not a problem for me. My father used to tell me I inherited my rage from my mother – we both were crowned with the virago's tell-tale tangle of fire-red hair – but I reckon he had more than a little to do with it. Eventually, when one particularly over-amorous lawyer made his advances, I stabbed him in the neck with a paperknife. He spent some time in the infirmary and it kicked up a fair old stink with my father. Before long, the truth of both my sex and my parentage was uncovered and my father left Ireland a disgraced man – with my birth mother and me in tow – to start a new life in Charles Town, Carolina.

That first day of our voyage to the colonies sticks clear and sharp in my memory, like the pleasure-pain prick of a hatpin. It is a memory almost as sharp as the first time I saw Mary.

Have you ever crawled up the bowsprit, at the very foremost point of a schooner? The ocean is all you can see. All you can smell and hear. A five-foot scooch backwards and the topsail and fore rigging will surround you. But sit up at the tip of the bowsprit and there is nothing but unsullied water all around.

I remember straddling it on that day, my boots crossed tight underneath at the ankles, watching two dozen gulls dip and swoop above my head, my eyes squinting in the afternoon sun. Looking out over the vast ocean, the wind whipping at my curls, I felt like a bird myself. I felt free. I felt like home.

2

My father practised the law for a while without much success, before finding his fortune in merchandise and buying a plantation in Charles Town. After losing him to his trade and my mother to a fever, my unruly reputation only grew. Increasingly drawn to the sea, I frequented the taverns in Charles Town's port: drinking, swiving and fighting with the seafaring men I found there. Eventually, I took a shine to a smart sailor by the name of James Bonny, who dragged me from a fight in an alehouse and allowed me to stow away on his voyages, upon my insistence of course.

James was poor, and somewhat dull, but his livelihood fostered my passion for the ocean. Within a month he had proposed, much to my father's fury. My father tried to straighten me out by matching me with a fine young man with a good reputation and a large inheritance, but I beat that fellow to within the last fingerbreadth of his life when he tried to lay with me against my wishes. I married James in secret soon after. When my father uncovered our marriage, he disowned me. In a blind rage, I set fire to his plantation, and James and I fled Charles Town on a schooner sailing to Nassau, New Providence.

New Providence was a filthy, lawless island, full of ramshackle inns and brothel houses, bursting at its seams with pirates, prostitutes and privateers. All were out for themselves. I fell in love with it immediately. I soon began spending all my time in the alehouses and brothels that lined Nassau Port, much to the annoyance of my new husband who had secured respectable employment helping to clean up the island under the new royal governor, Captain Woodes Rogers. As a former privateer, Rogers was seen as a traitor and despised by all the pirates I knew, including one I became particularly friendly with, Captain Jack Rackham.

***

I met Jack during a tornado that ripped through Nassau in June of 1719 when most ne'er-do-wells were taking shelter in Sal's Tavern, a popular alehouse and brothel. A regular there, I was never short of a drink, nor of company.

"Well, aren't you a long drink on a hot day?" were Jack's first words to me. He was dressed in a colourful calico patchwork dress coat and a tricorn hat. His handsome face was deep brown and furrowed from years on the open sea.

"A hot day?" I said, looking out to the storm. "You must be liquored already mister...the devil's pissing on Nassau, ain't he?"

He flashed a grin at me. At least two of his teeth were pure gold. "It's always sunny in Sal's, darlin'."

The large group of men assembled around him banged their tankards on the tables and chanted: "Sal's! Sal's! Sal's!".

I leant against the bar and surveyed him, my interest piqued, owing to his charm and the clear loyalty of his companions.

"Do people always agree with you, Mister…?"

"Rackham, *Captain* Jack Rackham. Some call me Calico Jack," he replied, his eyes glinting with pure amusement. "And everyone tends to agree but you, I reckon. What's your name, lass?"

"Anne."

"Just Anne?"

"Well, let's see. I came out of my mother as Anne Elizabeth Mary Cormac, if you require all of my particulars, but nowadays I go by Anne Bonny, on account of my husband."

Jack looked around the tavern, bemused. "And where is this…*husband?*"

"My husband is attached to me in law alone, Mister Rackham. He certainly has no say over my whereabouts." I looked him up and down. "And no man ever shall."

He let out a loud, hearty guffaw. "Well, well, you are a Bonny-Anne indeed. And ooh-ee, a lit barrel of gunpowder to boot." He reached into his top pocket and pulled out a single gold doubloon. I had never seen one before. "Care for a drink, Bonny-Anne?"

"Since you asked, Mister Rackham," I said, taking a seat on the nearest chair and swinging both feet up on to a table, crossed at the ankles. "As it happens, I am feelin' mighty parched."

I spent every day with Jack over the next fortnight, drinking and quarrelling our way around Nassau Port. Together we rode out the storm from both the tornado and my husband, from whom we had to hide during his almost daily hunts to find me — a futile effort to tow me back into line.

Jack and I became fast friends, then convenient lovers. We fought like cat and dog, but I confess I liked him more than any man before, or since. When the sun came out, I boarded a stolen sixty-foot sloop named *William* with Jack and his crew and never looked back.

3

I had been at sea on the *William* for two months and five days when I first set eyes on Mary Read. At first, I looked on her as a man – she went by the name of Mark at the time – but still, her effect on me was immediate.

We had just taken a sloop off Tortuga island, a small single-masted vessel. Our usual tactic on the open sea had prevailed: using my good self as a distraction. It was my idea of course. Women were rarely seen at sea – having a female aboard was widely considered to be bad luck – and I relished taking centre stage, inventing all sorts of shenanigans to confuse and mystify our enemy. With such an unusual spectacle surprising our opponents, we often found smaller ships easy to overcome.

Over the weeks I had gone from standing completely naked with a skull in one hand and a cutlass in the other; to swinging from the rigging and hollering like I belonged in an madhouse; to dancing a merry jig around the foresail in a flowing, bloodstained white robe. These theatrical displays were the only times I wore women's garments aboard the *William*. Dresses were ridiculous and completely impractical, and I did not need to remind the crew any more than necessary of my underlying femininity. Being a woman in a man's world is always problematic.

One of my most memorable and elaborate diversions was when I lashed a headless dressmaker's dummy to the bow, its torso splashed liberally with pig's blood. As we approached a merchant ship, I stood over the dummy – doused in blood myself, for good effect – wielding a huge beheading axe and screaming like a banshee. The other ship's crew were so frightened they gave up without so much as an ahoy – some of them even jumped overboard, trying to make a swim for it before we had barely come close. Truth be told, most of the crew of the *William* had been spooked too. Some still kept their distance from me wherever possible. I suppose an unpredictable woman is a fearsome prospect for many a man.

This time, however, I decided to keep things simple. I positioned myself in the crow's nest as we came up alongside the sloop, dressed in a fine red velvet robe, with my bodice ripped wide open to reveal my bare breasts.

On this occasion, all but one of the sloop's crew surrendered without a fuss. One man, however, burst from a cabin with his sword and pistol drawn, ready to fight single-handed. He managed to cross the gangway onto the *William*, kill two of our men and wound three others before I swung down on the rigging line and landed soundly in front of him.

"Now, you wouldn't hurt a lady, would you, mister?" I said, with my hands cupping my breasts.

"There's nary a lady I know who dresses like that," he replied, breathless from his endeavours. His clear blue eyes were assured, strong, with a hint of amusement. He had high cheekbones and lustrous, wavy auburn hair. I thought him to be a very unusual-looking man.

"I don't suppose you've ever had the pleasure of knowing me, now, have you?" I replied, with the sweetest face I could muster.

"Sure enough, I don't suppose I have," he said, stowing his weapons in his belt.

He walked to me, then, his eyes never leaving mine. He unfastened the red sash from his shoulder, and slowly wrapped it around my chest, covering me up. He was as close as many a man had been before, but I had never felt quite like this from someone's nearness.

He seemed to *see* me…gentle, understanding, challenging and strong, and all at once.

My cockiness all but gone, I grew still and stared into his eyes, which seemed to darken to the colour of midnight under my gaze. I felt his fingers tie the sash behind my head and brush lightly against my neck. My heart thudded, matching a pulse I saw throbbing in his throat. Then he stepped back and graced me with a smile like sunshine after the fiercest of storms.

Jack appeared alongside me, both pistols levelled at the man's chest, a look of sheer amazement on his face.

"Well, blow me down," Jack said. "It ain't the first time I've seen a fella conch-struck by my Bonny-Anne, but I do believe it's the first time I've ever seen Bonny-Anne silenced. Can you tame the Kraken, too, son?"

Loud laughter rang out around the deck from the rest of the crew, who had gathered to watch. The man pulled his gaze away from me and had the good sense to join in with the mirth. As any good seafarer knew, once their vessel's crew was bettered, if they did not unite with the victors, they would soon be thrown overboard and used as target practice.

"What's your name, son?" said Jack, slipping his pistols into his belt.

"Mark Read."

"You're a fine fighter, Mark Read. Not too many a man who'd try taking on the *William* alone. Besides, anyone who can tame our Anne deserves recruitment."

Another ripple of laughter spread across the deck. I rolled my eyes and huffed out my displeasure, feeling the colour rise in my cheeks. Embarrassment was a new experience for me.

"The name's Captain Jack Rackham. Some call me Calico Jack," he said, ignoring me and extending his hand. "Seems we're in the market for a couple of new men, thanks to you. Our aim is simple: take small ships, avoid King's ships, drink and be merry." The crew erupted with their customary roar of approval. Jack smiled. "What do you say to joining our happy band, Mister Read?"

Mark slid his eyes to me for a moment then nodded, shaking Jack's hand. "I reckon I feel right at home already, Cap'n."

"Then welcome aboard."

Jack clapped Mark on the back and put an arm around his shoulders. The crew broke into cheers and rowdy calls went up for a rum punch welcome party that evening. It seemed this mysterious young man could indeed charm just about anyone.

The crew searched the sloop for booty, booze and food before we loaded her with the dead, set her alight and, finally, adrift. Night was falling and I stood with Mark, aft of the mainsail, watching the blazing ship recede into the distance. Some of the crew moved around the deck, lighting the ship's port, starboard, quarterdeck and forecastle lanterns in preparation for the evening's merriment. Mark held a five-stringed guitar and a knapsack he had brought on board with him and stood perfectly still at the taffrail, a picture of calm.

I took the time to study his profile. A warm offshore breeze whipped his hair around his face, more chestnut now in the dimming light. Candlelight from the lanterns flickered in his eyes. As he became aware of my gaze, a corner of his mouth lifted, revealing a tiny hollow in his smooth cheek.

"Have we met somewhere before, Mister Read?" I asked.

He shook his head, turning to me. "I'd remember."

4

In the weeks that followed, we sailed to Jamaica and scoured the harbours and inlets of the east and south of the island, taking seven or eight small crafts with few men and not much booty, but we plundered just enough supplies to keep us satisfied. A military man, Mark's fighting ability was a great advantage and he spent many hours teaching me to parry and lunge, vastly improving my swordsmanship. Our early lessons were a source of great amusement for the crew; Mark's calmness and physical grace pitted against my impatience and fiery temper proved hugely entertaining, especially for those who enjoyed seeing me bettered.

Our very first lesson took place on a beach in Hispaniola, just after our first take with Mark as part of the team. He had almost single-handedly won the fight for us and the crew were clamouring to shake his hand and congratulate him. Even Jack could not hide his admiration.

We had dropped anchor in a large sandy cove along the abandoned north-west coast of the island to take stock. It was late afternoon and the sun hung low and large over Cuba and the Windward Passage. Jack ordered six of the crew to row ashore in search of wood and water for the ship, including Mark and me. Once landed, we sent the other four lads off to collect firewood, while Mark and I trudged through the jungle to locate a water source. Mark seemed to be a born water diviner, too, and within an hour we had filled a dozen wineskins and hauled them back to the beach, to wait for the wood party to return. The tide was receding fast, revealing vast stretches of sea grass sprouting up from the sand, like whiskers on a smooth chin.

Not one to sit about and do nothing, Mark lugged the wineskins to our rowboat and began hauling the vessel over the wet sand towards the waterline, which was now around half a furlong from where we had landed. I caught up with him, took hold of the bow rope, and together we dragged the boat out to meet the tide. A minute or so had passed when Mark stopped suddenly with a sharp intake of breath and bent over.

"Anne, look here!"

I looked over to where he was crouched. Nestled in amongst the sea grass lay a huge conch shell. Mark picked it up and held it aloft, a magnificent grin stretching over his beautiful face.

"I've never seen one that big!" I exclaimed, like an utter simpleton. I felt my face prickle, embarrassed at my unguarded outburst. Thankfully, Mark did not seem to notice.

"I've never seen one at all," he said. "I've heard about them, though. This here's a queen conch. A very rare find. A very rare find indeed."

He turned the rough, spiralled exterior over to reveal a beautiful bright coral pink underbelly. He traced his slim fingers over the large glossy pink outer lip. A brown snail emerged from his hiding place, its huge pointed claw swiping at Mark's fingers. It seemed very odd to me that something so beautiful could accommodate something so ugly and aggressive.

Mark took a knife from his coat pocket and made short work of cutting the snail from its shell, thoroughly scraping out its crevices. He transferred the bulbous flesh to his knapsack.

"That'll be a good addition to tonight's meal," he said, beaming. He knelt and washed the shell in the warm waters, before standing and holding the conch out to me, like it was the most precious prize in the world. "For you."

"Oh!"

Delighted, I took the shell from him and turned it in my hands. I ran my fingertips in and around its many whorls and stroked the smooth, shiny inner surface.

"It's heavier than I thought it would be," I said. "And much more beautiful than any shell I've seen before."

"Every queen conch is beautiful on the outside. Sometimes, rarely mind, you find a pearl inside one. A priceless pink pearl. They are so very hard to find, and so very valuable."

Excited, I brought the shell's opening close to my face and peered inside the empty crevice, looking for hidden treasure.

Mark chuckled. "I already looked, Anne. Alas, we didn't get lucky this time."

I smiled ruefully up at him. He was watching me intently.

It occurred to me then that, somehow, he had relaxed me enough that I had been acting a little too soft for my liking. I placed the shell carefully on the wineskins in the rowboat and leant against the rail, acting as nonchalant as I could.

"You're quite the dark horse, ain't you Mister Read?" I said, kicking off my boots and paddling my feet in the warm, shallow waters.

"Whatever do you mean, Miss Bonny?"

"You know – master swordsman, water diviner, shell connoisseur. What other tricks do you have up your sleeve, one wonders?"

He laughed and shook his head. "I just like to get on with things, Anne. I don't make a fuss, is all. There's nowt special about me."

"Maybe. Maybe not. Still, I have been thinking I can maybe learn a thing or two from you."

"It'd be my pleasure, Miss Anne." He took off his tricorn and held it to his chest, bowing elaborately. "What service may I offer you first?"

"I want you to teach me to fight like you."

He laughed, a bright, musical sound that warmed me. "You would have to listen, Anne."

"I've got ears, don't I?"

"Sure enough."

He walked to me and drew my sword from my sash. I felt a pull in my centre and involuntarily took one step closer to him.

"Hold out your left hand," he said softly.

His breath smelled sweet, like apples and fine spices. I held my hand out, palm up, and he placed the centre of my sword on my hand, balancing the blade perfectly, parallel with the sand below.

"The first lesson you must learn is that you are your sword, and, in knowing that, you must always be balanced - mentally and physically - for your sword to become one with you."

Stepping back, he performed the same action with his own sword, levelling it on his palm, and sank into a deep lunge - balancing his body perfectly. His sword did not move a whisker during the whole manoeuvre. "Try it, Anne."

I copied him as best I could and was quietly pleased when my sword hardly wobbled in my hand.

"Room for improvement, but a good start."

"Damn near perfect, that was!" I retorted.

"Now, stay exactly where you are and flip your sword up, catching it with your fighting hand, like this." He flipped his sword up and over and caught it smoothly by the hilt with his right hand - still in a perfect lunge.

Cocky now, I tossed the sword up, too quickly, and sent it twirling away from me, missing the catch completely. It sank blade-first into the wet sand, and I lost my balance, toppling to the ground.

"For pity's sake," I huffed, brushing down my breeches. "What's all this throwin', twirlin' and catchin' nonsense? When do we get to fight *properly?*"

"You mustn't let your emotions take charge of your sword."

"I ain't. My sword wants to kill you."

"Your sword is an extension of you, Anne."

"Fine. Then *I* want to kill you."

"No, you don't, Anne. You want to learn."

"Stop saying Anne."

His eyes twinkled with mirth, and something I thought looked like admiration. "Your sword reacts best to discipline. To physical control. If you let your heart rule, you will lose the fight. Every battle is won with the head."

"Are you implying I ain't clever?" I challenged, jutting out my chin.

"I'm implying your passion overrules your cleverness, of which, by the by, I have absolutely no doubt. Now…prepare…breathe. And…*en garde.*"

He settled into an elegant half lunge and levelled his sword at my chest, completely still, ready to fight.

I pulled my boots back on, picked up my sword, assumed the lunge position, and for the first time in my life…I decided to listen.

We practised until the sun went down and the other lads returned. By the end of our session, I had improved immeasurably. Mark was so delighted with my progress that he insisted on teaching me every day on the ship from then on. I was more than happy to oblige; it was the perfect excuse to spend more time with him.

After watching a couple of our lessons on the main deck, many of the crew signed up to learn Mark's style of elegant swordsmanship too. Even Jack saw the benefit.

Feeling confident with our improved skills, we took a double-masted schooner with ease just south of Port Royal. Its plentiful booty and supplies kept us fed and watered for a whole month.

Our next take was not so easy.

5

It was early morning when we rounded the westernmost point of Jamaica into Orange Bay. A heavy mist hung over the water and the sun had not yet broken through. Although the coast must have been only a furlong from our ship, we could not make it out. The only sound was the faint flutter of the *Roger* overhead and the sea lapping at the hull as *William* sliced slowly through the water. They were my least favourite conditions to sail in – let alone attack a ship – but Jack insisted we needed another take that day as we were running short on supplies, and there was always a sloop in Orange Bay – seeing as it was the last mooring before Montego Bay and its bustling markets.

We did not reckon on finding three ships moored together.

Before we knew it, we were upon them, their masts looming high through the mist, like crosses on Golgotha. Mark and I stood next to each other on the forecastle along with most of the crew, ready for battle. I glanced at Mark and saw concern plain on his face. I looked back at Jack – at the helm – and his face held worry, too. But there was no turning back now.

Jack spun the wheel to bring us alongside the first ship and his urgent whisper reached us easily on account of the mist's thick silence: *"Stealthy take, lads!"*

We hoisted the gangways over the taffrail and crept quickly and quietly onto the first Spanish sloop. Its main deck was deserted; its crew no doubt still slumbering below decks.

"Take the crew's quarters," I murmured to the lads.

They stole away to the starboard doorway which led down below deck, leaving Mark and me up top. There was no noise but creaks from the main masts and muffled steps from the crew as they descended the stairs below us.

"Captain's quarters are open, Annie," Mark whispered.

I ignored the jolt of pleasure I felt from his term of endearment and followed his gaze. He was right: the door to what would be the captain's cabin lay wide open.

"Anyone on the helm?" I asked urgently.

"Not that I can see."

"Where are the barrelmen?"

Mark looked upwards to the crow's nest. "Nowt there."

"I don't like this one little –"

"AVAST!"

Out of the mist, three dozen men charged from the second ship alongside. They clambered over

36

gangways and swung down from rigging-lines armed with swords, grappling irons, and clubs. Instantly, Mark surged forwards with his sword drawn and took on the first of them.

"Main deck!" I hollered, hoping the crew could hear me.

I fired my pistol at the most dangerous-looking Spaniard I could see, who was armed with two flintlocks and a wild look in his eyes. A heart-stopping *booooom* thundered through my chest as a cannon fired behind me and tore through the oncoming crowd, eliminating at least five of the horde. Swirling sulphurous fumes and smoke filled my nostrils. My ears rang. Breathless, I looked behind me to see Jack lighting the second gun's fuse on the *William*. Then, with a rallying cry, he leapt over the taffrail to join the fight.

Cries echoed through the smoke and mist as the second cannonball hit the crowd. I fought on, slashing a neck, an arm, a face, another neck. My shirt clung to my chest with sweat and blood. Jack appeared next to me and fired both pistols into the melee before discarding them and drawing his cutlasses. Ahead, I could make out Mark's long blade swishing left and right, slashed with red.

Musket shots whistled through the air, heralding our crew's arrival from below decks. Panic broke out among the Spaniards when they realised they were now outnumbered. They started to retreat, jumping overboard to escape. Huge plumes of water splashed up and over the rails. Some of our crew ran to the taffrails and began picking them off in the water with their pistols, one by one. As the enemy dispersed, I looked around for Mark.

Beside me, Jack sneered. "Bloody Spaniards. Couldn't fight on their own, had to join with the other ships. Bloody coat-tail cowards."

I turned and punched him in the face, hard. He stumbled back, grasping his nose.

"Ahh! Anne – what the –"

"How many times have I told you? Never attack in the mist! Bloody Spaniards...? Bloody brainless, Jack. That's what you are."

I stalked off in a blind rage to find Mark. I found him on the sterncastle deck, hunched over, clutching at his side. My stomach dropped.

"You're hurt."

"It's just a scratch, Annie. Nowt to lose your head over."

He smiled at me and tried to stand up. His face twisted in pain. Moving closer, I gently lifted his hand away and opened his coat. His shirt was slashed open along his belly and a bright red patch bloomed through the cotton.

"Oh, bilge, Read. That there is no scratch. Let's get you back to quarters and fix you up."

I hoisted his other arm over my shoulder and walked him slowly back onto the *William*, glaring at Jack as we passed. He held a bandana to his bloody nose and eyed me warily.

"Search all ships for booty!" he barked to the crew.

"We'll be in captain's quarters," I called back to him.

"Bloody women," I heard him mumble.

6

I helped Mark out of his coat and onto the bed that Jack and I shared. His face was pale and covered with sweat. I began unbuttoning his shirt.

He grabbed my hand. "Annie, I'm fine. Leave me be, I just need to rest."

"Claptrap," I said, pushing his hands away. "You're still bleeding."

I popped another button. He gripped my wrists firmly, stilling them. His eyes held mine and, again, I felt our connection. That pull. Tugging me towards him from deep within my centre. I wondered briefly if he felt it as well.

I searched his eyes for an answer, leaning into him. He was so close I could see tiny golden flecks, like stars, in his ever-darkening blue eyes. His cheeks were flushed with colour. I dropped my eyes to his mouth, captivated by the way his lips swelled and parted.

"Annie —"

We were both breathing heavily. The air between us was charged, alive with energy. And then the only thought I had in my head, the only possible thing I could do in that moment, was to bring my mouth to his.

I had been kissed by many men before, but never had it felt like this. Melting, pillowy softness; feather-light, delicate, breathy kisses — slowly, tentatively exploring each other. As I moved to deepen the kiss, he brought his hand between us and gently pushed me away.

"Annie…there's something you should know."

My eyelids fluttered open. Dazed and breathless, I tried to focus on him. Blood roared in my ears.

"What is it?" My voice did not sound like my own. The words seemed to come out from somewhere very far away. I felt entirely disoriented, like my head was underwater; heavy, yet floating. "Is it Jack? You don't need to worry about him," I mumbled, dipping my head to kiss his neck. "I'm not his only paramour, you know."

"No, I —" He sat up straighter, wincing with the pain from his cut. He took a deep breath. "I think it's easier if I show you. Just...don't kill me, all right? Remember...I'm still me."

His hands moved to his shirt and he unfastened the last few buttons. Then, slowly, he pulled it open.

His skin underneath was smooth and milky white in contrast to the deep tan on his face and neck. My eyes moved lower and settled on two small, but unmistakeable breasts that heaved in and out. The breasts were tipped with rose-pink nipples, tight with arousal.

I sucked in a breath. "You're – you're a *woman?*"

Aghast, I clapped my hands over my mouth and stumbled back off the bed, onto the floor. She tried to swing her legs round to come to me but cried out in pain. A stream of blood seeped out of the cut on her ribs. I went to her, covering the cut with a bandana and pressing hard. We frantically searched each other's eyes for some understanding, a reconnection. She must have read downright confusion in mine because she reached for my hand and pressed it to her chest. With a deep, shuddering breath, she began to tell me her story.

"Annie. My real name is Mary Read. But I have lived as a man for as long as I can remember." She looked at me in earnest. "I never lied about who I am, just who I started out as. My mother disguised me as a boy when I was very young to guarantee my grandmother's support. And so, I became my elder

44

brother Mark, who died just before I was born. I have been him all my life. I was in the military for nine years before I boarded that sloop. Then I met you. Please understand…I never meant to hide anything from you. You know me better than anyone. This is who I am."

She lifted her hand slowly and brought it to my face, cupping my cheek and swiping a single tear away with her thumb. I instinctively turned my face into her hand and kissed her palm. Her eyebrows rose slightly, and she gazed at me, waiting for me to respond.

"So…it's Mary, is it?" I said, a small smile tugging at my lips.

"It's anything you like, Annie."

Her expression was so sincere, so loving, that I found myself overcome with emotion, and wondered briefly at this strange, new, soft person that I had become.

I leant in and kissed her shyly, exploring her again, almost as if it were the first time.

Gentle, almost chaste kisses quickly made way for more. I opened my mouth to deepen the kiss and she moaned, pushing her tongue into my mouth. Her fingers moved up into my hair to clutch a fistful of curls. We moved together instinctively, pushing and pulling at each other with increased desperation, as if we were the only things holding each other up.

More. All I could think was, *I need more.*

I wanted to breathe her in, to consume her.

I sucked her bottom lip in between my teeth, bit along her jawline, and kissed hungrily down the smooth column of her neck. I was just moments away from unbuttoning her breeches when approaching footsteps broke us apart.

Mary pushed me away quickly and closed her shirt, settling back onto the bed, her face flushed, her chest heaving. I grabbed the bloody bandana and pressed it to her, trying to calm my own ragged breathing and pounding heart.

The cabin door was thrown wide open and Jack strode in. "How's the patient?"

"He'll survive –" "I'll live –" we said in unison.

We stared at each other, our eyes wide. We could barely conceal our amusement at the situation, like two children caught with their hands in the gingerbread pot.

"Glad to hear it, Bucko."

Jack tossed a sack of what sounded like coins onto the captain's table and leant up against the bedpost, oblivious to our flustered state.

"You can patch me up next, Anne," he said, pinching the bridge of his bloodied nose. "I'll forgive you for this, by the by – just this once, mind – but only because we've plundered more Spanish doubloons than I reckon even Governor Rogers has in his filthy, double-crossin' coffers. Not only that, but enough rum, mead, cured meats and beans to keep us alive for a month. And *live chickens*, would you believe! *Chickens!* Tonight, my friends, we celebrate."

L ater that afternoon, we dropped anchor just outside Montego Bay and welcomed aboard three of Jack's acquaintances whom he had sent for, taxied from the harbourside in the ship's rowboat: Pierre the dressmaker (who dressed even more elaborate than Jack in frilly-edged shirts and a pink coat), Matthew the barber, and another tall, smart gentleman named Alasdair whom I had not met before. Pierre and Matthew took those of the crew who required servicing and smartening up in captain's quarters, including Jack himself. Mary declined the offer, of course, flashing a conspiratorial smile in my direction.

After a slap-up meal below decks of chicken and bean stew, accompanied by enough rum and mead to sink a galleon, the party spilled up onto the deck and we danced the day away. The crew sang their usual work shanties, swaying backwards and forwards, arms wrapped around each other, bottles sloshing:

Come all ye young fellows that follows the sea,
Way hey, blow the man down,
Now please pay attention and listen to me,
Oh, give us some time to blow the man down.

Even though they were all blind drunk, the crew could still carry a tune.

By sundown, the whole ship was sluiced except for Mary and me. I was so distracted by her whereabouts all day that I had taken in a mere fraction of my normal booze consumption. Mary had pretended to muster up as much enthusiasm as the rest of the crew in their merriment, but her eyes had met mine so often – clear, intense and gunpowder-sharp – that I knew she too had been afflicted with the same malady.

At one point, Jack staggered over to me and threw an arm around my shoulders. He brought his mouth close to my ear, meaning to whisper but failing miserably in his drunken stupor.

"Anne! Come to quarters for a wee while, will yer? I needs to show yer somethin'."

His breath was ripe with the stench of chewing tobacco and alcohol, and the gold-toothed grin I used to find quite charming now felt overpowering and repellent. I dipped my head to sneak a sideways glance at Mary. She was staring cold-bloody-murder at Jack. For some reason this made me ridiculously pleased.

"Ahh, not tonight, Jack," I said lightly. "There's a party we'll be missin' out on."

Unperturbed, Jack threw his other arm around Pierre, the next man in line, so we were all part of one long conjoined set. He took a long swig from the bottle of rum dangling from the hand draped over my chest and slurred out his favourite self-penned shanty, singing at the top of his lungs:

Oh, give me a kiss Bonny-Anne!
Oh, send me one fast as ye can.
All the sailors at sea, are conch-struck by thee!
So, give me a kiss Bonny-Anne!

He grabbed my face and kissed me roughly. Mildly annoyed, I shoved him away and the entire line of men collapsed in a heap of drunken laughter. They rolled around on the deck, embracing one another, singing another verse of my song and clinking their bottles together.

Eventually, the ship began to quieten down. The men sat huddled in groups against the ship's hull, chatting and chuckling quietly or snoring with their mouths wide open.

I positioned myself directly opposite Mary, who sat with her back against the mainmast, her guitar cradled in her lap.

"Come now, Mark," said Pierre, resting his head on Jack's shoulder. "Are yer goin'ta sing us a shanty with that there thing? The party's dyin', man."

I did not think Mary would comply, but she offered a quick smile and began to play. Her graceful fingers moved up and down the neck of the guitar, plucking out a sweet, melancholy tune.

A hush descended on the ship as those left awake turned to listen to the beautiful music under the lantern light. Then, as clear and strong as a church bell, Mary began to sing:

I once saw an angel at sea,
Her wings unfurled only for me,
She swooped o'er the isles, and I watched her, beguiled,
As she showed me the meaning of free.

My sea angel guides me through storms,

She leads me from cold seas to warm,
When my angel is near, I've no place for fear,
Sure as after the night comes the dawn.

She was so beautiful I could hardly breathe.

I felt a sudden sharp stab of fear. I had never been in love before. I felt weak, exposed, full, strong. And utterly terrified.

***

One by one, the crew made their way below decks to turn in for the night. Among them were Jack and Pierre, arm in arm, laughing and whispering in their own merry world. Mary raised her eyebrows at me in surprise, and I laughed.

"I told you I wasn't his only paramour."

Finally, Mary and I were left alone on the deck.

Our eyes met and we rose immediately, striding towards each other, our lips meeting in a bruised, heated kiss. I tried to convey all the emotion I was feeling with that kiss. By some miracle, I felt her deliver the same love letter to me.

Hand in hand, we walked up the stairway to the quarter deck – where we knew we would be hidden from anyone returning from crew's quarters – and settled down against the helm.

Mary wrapped me securely in her arms, my back against her chest.

We both let out deep sighs of satisfaction.

"Tell me more about yourself," I said.

"Ask me anything."

"Have you ever been married?"

"Yes."

I turned sharply in her arms. *"What?* To *whom?"* I demanded. A hot, heavy rock of jealousy lodged itself deep in my chest. "Tell me his name so I can find him and kill him."

Mary laughed quietly and pulled me closer. "His name was Marcel and he died two years ago. We served in the army together. We bunked together in the field, so he discovered my sex eventually. Marcel was a great friend to me; we had a lot of good times. After the war, we even opened an inn together. But…honestly, I never realised there *was* an alternative to men. Until you."

I felt the rock dislodge and fall away.

"Very well then," I said, settling back against her.

She chuckled and kissed my temple. After a while, she said: "Are you ready to retire, Annie?"

"No, not yet," I replied softly. "I'm not ready at all."

"Would you like a drink?"

"No. I want to remember every moment."

I tilted my head to breathe into the crook of her neck and ran my fingers gently over her chest. She smelled of the sea. Of comfort, adventure. Of infinite promise.

I kissed the underside of her chin and felt her shudder. She blew out a shaky breath.

"You make me lose all thought, all control," she whispered. "This could be dangerous for us."

"How can it be dangerous when it feels as natural as breathing?"

She shifted on the deck to face me and took my hands in hers. I intertwined our fingers tightly.

"You are a very rare creature, Anne Bonny. I am so lucky to have found you."

I hesitated before asking, "As rare as a queen conch?"

"Oh yes. You are more rare and *much* more beautiful than a queen conch. And infinitely more precious than its pearl."

I was amazed and fascinated by this revelation.

"You seem to behold me rather differently than other folk," I scoffed quietly.

"You don't show yourself to them," she said simply.

"No. Only you."

"Only me?"

"Yes. Only you."

We talked through the night; imparting our histories, making plans and sharing dreams, until sunlight bled through the line where the sky met the sea. Together, we watched the sun rise on a new day, both knowing everything had changed for us. Neither admitting how difficult it might turn out to be.

8

I led Mary back towards quarters, feeling light and free despite the stiffness in my body from hours of sitting on the hard deck.

"Come to bed with me, Mary."

She looked at me, surprised.

"Annie. Jack will be awake soon enough and then, sure enough, he will be up these stairs to return to you. Another night."

I knew she was right. With a sigh of resignation, I kissed her.

"Very well. Goodnight, Mary."

"Good *morning*, Annie. It *was* a good night. Get some rest."

She ran her fingertips along my jaw one last time and tiptoed down the stairwell to the crew's quarters.

As quietly as I could, so as not to wake Jack and the crew below, I opened the door to captain's quarters. The welcome sight of the empty bed made me realise how exhausted I was.

I had just begun to undress when I felt a heavy thump to the back of my head, and everything went black.

***

When I awoke, I could not see nor move. My head was pounding as if it had been split in two. I quickly took stock: both my hands and feet were tied tightly. A rough gunny sack covered my head. I heard distant gulls and felt a familiar pitch and roll and knew instinctively that I was inside a moving vessel at sea, but it was not the *William*. I managed to wriggle myself up into a sitting position.

"She's awake," a voice said.

Two sets of footsteps approached.

"Take the sack off."

Light filled my vision. My eyes took a moment to adjust.

Before me, in a small cabin filled with barrels and wineskins, stood my estranged husband, James Bonny, and Alasdair – the smart gentleman who had boarded the *William* with Pierre's party yesterday. Or was it more than one day ago? I had no idea.

"You filthy *mudsuckers!*" I rasped, my throat dry and painful. I struggled fiercely against my trussed hands and feet, to no avail.

James fetched a pitcher of water and sloshed some into my mouth. It spilled over my cheeks and dripped down my chest. I sucked in as much as I could.

"Do be calm, Anne. You're safe now."

"Be calm? *Be calm!* You kidnapped me, James, you *cowardly pig!*"

"Nonsense. You are my wife. One cannot kidnap one's own wife."

61

They laughed as if we were at some sort of posh high tea party and I was not tied up, half-dressed and sodden on the floor.

"You're mad," I said.

"Not in the least. You are my wife, my property. I simply employed Mr Tandy here to help recover what is mine."

"When you untie me, I am going to kill you."

"With what weapons Anne, dear? Your bare hands? You may be wearing gentlemen's attire but unless I'm sorely mistaken you are still just a *woman*."

More laughter.

I felt my rage building and welcomed her in like an old friend.

"*Ha!* What on earth is this twattery-fakery way of talkin' you have now? Tryin'a speak and act like a gentleman when we both know all you are is a failed halfpenny-pirate-turned-snitch who can't even keep his own cock up, let alone keep his wife in line. Gov'nor Rogers has certainly done some work on you, James. And it ain't for the better, let me tell you. Done you up like a stinkin' kipper in a suit, with a stick right up yer arse. He surely has."

James's face turned beetroot. I smiled. It was nice to know I still riled him up as much as I always did.

"You will *not* disrespect me any longer, Anne!" he thundered. "If I cannot keep you *in line*, as you say, then a public flogging from the governor will. And as soon as we are docked in Nassau, that is what you shall receive. So, I suggest you gather your strength, my darling wife. You will need it."

A frisson of fear coiled in my belly: slow, cold and heavy, like an anchor's chain.

I did not let it show.

Instead, I shut my mouth in a stubborn, firm line and refused to look at or talk to James for the remainder of our journey. I decided it was in my best interest to keep quiet and not make the situation any worse. I ate the food and drink that was offered, slept, and thought of nothing else but Mary, and my impending fate.

9

New Providence looked nothing like I remembered.

There were no beaten-up, filthy pirate sloops anchored haphazardly in the bay. Only pristine merchant navy ships, smartly tethered to newly constructed jetties in Nassau Port; Saint George's flags fluttering brightly overhead; sails gleaming white. Gone were the rickety old market stalls along the harbourside, selling stolen booty. Instead, half a dozen painted horse carts were neatly lined up, offering baked goods, milk and eggs, fruit and vegetables, woven baskets and the like. No prostitutes and pirates lurked in the tavern doorways or on street corners, only King's Guards who marched the streets in pairs, stopping to talk with gentlemen in suits and ladies in bonnets and pretty summer dresses. The cobbled streets where I had spent many a drunken day were clean of barrels, bodies and bottles, and I could not spot one fight spilling out of the newly whitewashed taverns. I could not detect even the slightest whiff of sulphur, alcohol or tobacco in the air.

It seemed Governor Rogers' clean-up mission had been a success.

"Isn't Nassau a pretty sight now, Anne?" James said, cautiously edging closer to me on the deck.

On our approach, he had asked Alasdair to dress me in an ivory silk robe and tie my wrists to the foremast to stop me from lashing out, as I had on many occasions over the past few days. Underneath his perfectly pressed dress shirt and tunic, I suspected James was black and blue.

"Yes," I replied. "I hate it."

He ignored me and rocked on his heels, puffing out his chest like a proud frigate bird. "I think you'll be most taken with Governor Rogers' mansion. He converted the old wooden fort on Fitzwilliam Hill into a beautiful residence. He had the quarried stone shipped all the way from Kentucky! It's even bigger than your father's was in Charles Town."

James pointed up to the hill behind Nassau Port where a huge stone house with four stout white columns stood. The windows were framed with white wooden louvre shutters and the exterior walls had been painted a bright conch-pink. It made me think of Mary.

"You've been careless in forgetting I don't care nothin' for life on land, James. You have wasted your time and mine by bringing me back here. My life is at sea. Back where you found me."

"Nonsense. I am convinced there is a lady in you. You come from good stock, Anne. You need pulling back into line, that's all." He put a careful arm around my waist, and I twisted, jamming my elbow as hard as I could into his side. He yelped in pain and stepped quickly away from me.

"I've told you before," I spat. "Get your filthy, traitorous snitch-fingers *off* me."

With that, James turned on his heel and marched away to join Alasdair, who was overseeing our docking harbourside.

"She'll come around," I heard him say, with what sounded like a little less conviction than before.

***

In the crowded courtroom, I saw Woodes Rogers right away.

He sat in an ornate high-backed chair at the very front, behind a huge raised wooden desk. A black dress coat strained tight against his belly – I could see his white shirt through the gaping holes between his buttons – exposing a life of luxury and excess. He wore a ridiculously large judicial wig on his head, which I reckoned must have been made from at least five horses' tails. I decided that he most likely wore one that big to help conceal his puffy red face.

Rogers was some twenty yards away, but I could feel his eyes on me as I approached. I wondered how many people he judged in this place every day. And how few people he spared.

James left me to take his place in the public gallery to one side and Alasdair led me to the front of the courtroom, my hands still bound tightly. As we walked, people on both sides swivelled in their seats and craned their necks to inspect me, whispering and tutting disapprovingly to one another. I recognised some of them as old acquaintances.

I tried to act as nonchalant as possible.

Inside, I felt like a fish out of water, gasping for breath.

I did not belong here. These people, this place, and everything I had left behind felt so suffocating, so unfamiliar to me now. I felt my old self clambering back up from somewhere deep within me. I suppose she was the only defence I had left to summon.

"Gov'nor Woodes Rogers. It's surely a *pleasure* to meet you," I said, as sunny and bright as a day in May.

Rogers appraised me with a strange mixture of intense disdain and complete indifference. It reminded me of the way my father used to look at me. Like a hawk inspecting an insect from someplace high above.

He plucked a long, elaborate quill from an inkpot, scratched out something in a huge leather-bound book and began to speak. His voice was high, thin and reedy, quite the opposite to his appearance. I fought an urge to giggle.

"Anne Elizabeth Mary Bonny. You are accused by your husband, James Bonny, of committing adultery with one Jack Rackham. You are also accused by the New Providence government of conspiring to steal the merchant navy sloop *William* from Nassau Port on July fourteenth, in the year of our Lord seventeen hundred and nineteen. Do you confess to these crimes?"

I took a quiet, steadying breath, pushed out my chin and forced myself to look directly into Rogers' cold eyes. Then I smiled sweetly.

"If you are asking me: did I have sexual relations with the famous Captain Jack Rackham, then yes I did. But there's somethin' you got wrong. I did not have sexual relations with just the one fella, you see…I couldn't really count 'em on my own fingers, if we're really s'posed to be honest in this place, Gov'nor."

James began a small coughing fit on the other side of the courtroom. The crowd whispered excitedly, twittering like mockingbirds. I continued, beginning to enjoy inhabiting my old self again.

"If you are asking me: did I steal a boat with the said Captain Jack Rackham, then yes, I did. But I did not just steal a boat. Truth be told, there's not a lot of things I *haven't* stolen these past months. Although, I s'pose you most likely feel I am a kindred spirit, *Mister* Rogers. Word has it you've taken your fair share of things that aren't yours, too. From what I hear, anyways."

There was a collective gasp from the courtroom. James's face was beginning to turn purple.

The governor's face was calm, impassive, impenetrable.

"Mrs Bonny. I am sorry to say that your sources are sorely mistaken. With the company you keep, this is no surprise. I will thank you to only speak of facts and relay the truth in my courtroom."

"Governor," James said, finally finding his voice from across the room, "please excuse my wife. I regret to say she has always been considered *simple* in polite company. She did not receive a proper

72

education, so she lacks the intellect to understand what she is saying or doing in these situations. I must apologise on her behalf for her idiocy and insubordination. She is in my care now, and I will be sure to remedy her behaviour as soon as possible."

Rogers did not even bother to look up from his writings. "Well, for reasons quite unknown to me, it seems your husband cares enough to have saved your hide, Mrs Bonny. You are a lucky woman. You have him and him alone to thank for keeping you out of jail. Therefore, following your husband's claim on you, and your own…*rather candid*…confessions, I hereby grant you the King's Pardon, on the condition that you change your sinful ways. However –" he paused to look at me, his fat lips twitching with the slightest suggestion of pleasure. "– as governor of this civilised British colony, I simply cannot allow your public infidelity and debauchery to go unpunished. I therefore sentence you to twenty-one lashes in the town square, tomorrow at noon. After which, you are free to leave and return with your husband to his estate. Where, I would suggest, Mr Bonny," he said, finally turning his attention to my pathetic husband, "you work on your wife's rehabilitation and her eventual reintegration into our civilised society."

"Yes, your Honour – er, yes, *Governor*. I plan to do precisely that. Thank you for your understanding and leniency with regards to my wife's inexcusable behaviour. It is very much appreciated."

If James had his tongue any further up Rogers' arse, he would be eating the governor's supper for him.

Rogers continued as though James had said nothing. "If, however, I receive word that Mrs Bonny's promiscuous tendencies have resurfaced, I shall have no hesitancy in throwing her in jail pending a full trial and punishment, as is deemed appropriate under the King's Law. Is this understood, Mr Bonny?"

"Understood," James almost whimpered.

I rolled my eyes.

"Mrs Bonny?" Rogers looked at me, his quill poised to write something else in his big fat book.

"I s'pose," I replied, shrugging my shoulders.

"Very well. Take her away, Mr Tandy. And Mr Bonny, Mr Tandy – be sure to present Mrs Bonny to the town square by noon tomorrow for her whipping."

Next to me, Alasdair nodded, rose silently and led me out of the courtroom, his vice-like grip burning into my forearm. James scurried out from the cheap seats and followed behind us, making sure he was always well out of my reach, of course.

I have never prayed to any god, but as I was dragged from that courthouse, I offered up a silent plea that – somehow – I would get the chance to wreak my revenge on these cowardly, pitiful excuses for men.

Sometime soon.

10

The next morning, an open horse-drawn carriage was waiting outside James's house to take me to the town square for my public humiliation.

Alasdair took charge of dressing me again, most likely knowing that if I were left with a handmaiden, I would make my escape. I wondered what plans they were making to ensure that could never happen, and clung to the hope that – one day, for just one moment – they would become complacent. That was all I required.

Alasdair silently washed me from head to toe in a cast iron bathtub – my hands trussed to an eye hook in the ceiling and his hands roaming wherever they pleased. Afterwards, he dressed me in a simple thin white cotton gown, but with no undergarments. I tried not to think of the reasons why. Then he led me outside, to where James waited by the open carriage. My husband had a strange, satisfied look on his face. It was almost as if he were enjoying this, much as one would a special occasion. Not for the first time, I thought he must have some sort of profound mental retardation to conclude that the public whipping of his wife was an event to be celebrated. Or to think that I would somehow emerge miraculously transformed into a subservient wife.

I looked up at the cloudless blue sky, taking my mind somewhere far away, searching for some comfort. A lone herring gull circled high overhead, its cries echoing off the hillside. I tracked its journey from land to sea, out towards a small lugsail fishing boat returning from its morning catch. Gulls surrounded its yellowing sails, two dozen fluttering white dots in the distance.

It was the most perfect sailing day, calm waters and steady winds. The sun glittered a path over the ocean, its rays reflecting a thousand times upon gleaming waves of water, taunting me with a narrowing, sparkling route of escape; a clear course set for Mary, so very far beyond the horizon.

"Come now, Anne," said James, cheerfully. "This day marks the end of your old life and the beginning of a new one with me. Together. Let us travel happily, *in peace*, from this moment on."

I did not dignify his nonsense with a reply. Instead, I took his offered hand and stepped up into the carriage silently. I sat in the coach with James and Alasdair squeezed tight on either side of me. A rose between two pricks.

***

As we made our way into town, I understood why the governor had sent an *open* carriage.

People lined every street.

And not just men. Women and children filled the cobblestones in their hundreds, all of them dressed in brightly coloured suits and summer frocks. It seemed to me that there was a considerable number of women, especially. They gathered in excited groups, standing on tiptoe, pointing at me and gossiping with one another, every one of them straining for a good look at the infamous lady pirate.

Groups of girls played with whittled wooden sticks, pretending they were sword fighting. One little lass even had her dress tucked into her stockings to make it look as if she was wearing breeches. She swished her pretend sword left and right, a handkerchief tied around her mop of unruly, bright red hair. As our carriage passed, I caught her eye and smiled. It was the first time I had truly smiled in days. Her mother stepped in front of her, admonishing the girl and pulling her dress free before anyone else could notice.

79

It felt like I was in the middle of a grand wedding procession. And I was the bride.

Then a thought struck me: not only was I the first female pirate anyone had ever heard of, but I was most likely the first woman anyone had seen publicly whipped.

Usually, few people attended floggings. They had been such a commonplace occurrence on land for so long, that those present generally consisted of the culprit, his guardian or master and the guards tasked with carrying out the punishment. And maybe a drunk or two.

It seemed I had single-handedly made whippings a popular spectator pastime again.

The driver slowed the horse from a trot to a walk and the line of people street-side began to deepen.

We had arrived.

I peered past the driver's shoulder as he brought the carriage to a complete stop.

In the centre of the town square, roped off from the crowd of onlookers, stood a tall wooden whipping post on a raised stone platform. The stage was flanked by a pair of King's Guards dressed in their customary red, white and black uniforms. One of the guards was armed with a long rifle, capped with a gleaming bayonet. The other held a cat o' nine tails whip at his side.

My stomach flipped and dropped heavily into my groin.

A cat o' nine tails!

Lashings were usually administered using the single-tailed whip, either a single rope's end or a leather cord used for horses and the like. Not at all pleasant, but overnight I had imagined the pain would be manageable. I was used to injury, to hurting.

The cat o' nine tails, however, was an entirely different prospect. It was reserved for the punishment of the most severe offenders. A short

81

whip, with nine knotted strands of rope connected to its handle, it was said to make you feel as though you were being lashed with nine whips made from sharp rocks, all at the same time. Whipping sentences were set in groups of three, up to a maximum of thirty-nine lashes. Men had died from the blood loss that came with thirty-nine lashes of a cat o' nine tails.

As I climbed down from the carriage, I frantically tried to remember the sentence I had been given. I had been so intent on antagonising the governor and James in the courtroom that I had barely taken any notice of the formalities.

Had he said *twenty-one* lashes? For a *woman?* With a *cat o' nine tails?*

For the first time ever, I feared for my life.

Silence fell on the town square as Alasdair and James ushered me towards the whipping post. There were no children playing here. The raffish crowds on the outskirts of town had given way to a higher class of spectator: wealthy landowners, their wives well clad in the latest fashions. Up close, the women lining the square found it harder to look me in the eye, their heads bowing as I was led past. One group had lined up close to the platform, yet were so prudish that they hid their faces within their deep-brimmed summer bonnets, twitching the hems of their long dark cloaks as if to pull them as far as possible from my path. Opposite them stood a group of older men and women, all dressed in black and white – I knew most of them as the colony's elders. They looked at me with a queer mixture of interest and pity. It was just a small measure away from satisfaction. No wonder James felt so at home here.

We reached the stage and James left to join the elders. Alasdair pulled me onto the platform, dragging me over to the whipping post.

"Allow me, Mrs Bonny," he murmured, very close to my ear.

He lifted my trussed wrists above my head and tied them to a metal ring nailed high on the post.

Then he crouched and removed my silk slippers, squeezing my ankles spitefully. I felt him tie my feet together tightly. He tethered that rope to another ring at the foot of the pole. Then he straightened and used a knife to cut through the delicate shoulders of my dress. The gown parted and slipped away from me, leaving me completely naked.

I heard gasps from the crowd. And a low chuckle from Alasdair as he left my side.

Behind me, the guard's footsteps were approaching.

I felt wetness on my cheeks and realised I was crying. I rested my forehead against the wood between my arms, squeezed my eyes shut, and braced myself for the agony that was sure to follow.

"AVAST!"

Gunshots rang out. Two loud musket shots, close to me. A rifle shot. Then five, six, seven more musket shots. Metal clanged against metal. Grunts and groans. Warm liquid splashed on my back, ran down my legs. I whipped my head to the left. To the right. I could not see anything from under my arms. But I could hear women screaming and men shouting. People jostling, running away. I could smell gunpowder. And blood…I could smell blood.

And then, suddenly, someone was close behind me, breathless and hot.

I braced myself.

Then I smelled something else. Apples and fine spices.

"*Annie!* Annie! Are you all right?"

Mary.

Mary had come for me.

She circled me, frantically cutting my hands and feet loose before taking my face in her hands. Her eyes were wild; incandescent with rage, the rush of blood, and some kind of raw, unbridled intensity that I had never seen in her before; that I had never seen directed at me before.

Worry. Love.

It was then that I noticed the summer bonnet tied about her neck and the black cloak that now draped like a cape down her back. She untied the cloak, wrapped it around my body, and handed me a short sword from her belt.

"Let's get out of here, Annie."

I turned and took in the scene before me.

Only a dozen people were left standing in the square. Nearly all the crowd had dispersed. A score of men lay dead or dying on the cobblestones. Unfortunately, as far as I could make out, none of them looked to be James or Alasdair.

Both King's Guards lay next to each other in front of Mary and me, their throats slashed, a bullet hole in one's chest. Dark pools of blood expanded and met underneath them, turning the limestone below almost black.

In the square, Jack and five or six of the crew were seeing off any brave – or stupid – men who had chosen to stay and fight. The crew were easy to spot – ladies' summer bonnets dangled from their necks.

I examined the men that had stayed to fight. James was not among them. *Of course. Pathetic.*

Then I spotted Alasdair.

He was doing his best to fight Jack off, using the dead guard's rifle bayonet as a weapon.

I leapt off the stage and ran at him.

"Annie!" Mary yelled.

Alasdair turned his head and watched, his eyes wide, as I raced towards him, Mary's black cloak billowing out behind my naked, blood-streaked body. I must have looked a real fright because even Jack did a double take before he took the opportunity to disarm Alasdair, pinning his arms behind his back and pushing him down onto his knees.

"Allow *me*, Mr Tandy," I said, and slashed my sword across his throat.

Blood cascaded down the front of his pristine suit. He looked at me in amazement for one delicious moment. I inhaled sharply and launched a thick gob of spit onto his face. His eyes rolled up into his head, and he slumped to the ground, face-first.

Mary arrived at my side and placed a hand on my shoulder.

"I never did like that fella," Jack said, breathlessly. "Dresses like a pettifogger. And he always cheats at cribbage."

11

We knew it was only a matter of minutes before the governor received word of what had happened and sent the King's Guard out in full force. We wasted no time in getting out of the square.

"Where are we going? Where's the *William*?" I asked Mary as we chased Jack and the crew down side streets and alleyways. As we ran, we tied bonnets around our heads and concealed our weapons. I used Mary's sash to tie my cloak tight around my waist.

"Anchored in Goodman's Bay," Mary replied breathlessly.

I knew it well – a wide, sandy bay two miles west of Nassau Port, as the crow flies.

"We're heading to Sal's Tavern first...apparently you know it?" Mary continued, glancing at me. "We stole four horses from Goodman's Farm to get us here; they're tied up in the alley behind the tavern."

"Mark!" Jack hollered ahead of us. "Stop your jabbering and make Anne run faster! I am not dyin' today!"

"I've got no bleedin' shoes on, you old fool!" I yelled. But I ran faster anyway.

***

We managed to reach Sal's undetected, and rode double pillion cross-country to Goodman's Farm. I rode behind Mary, my arms wrapped tight around her waist. As we galloped over the countryside, I caught glimpses of the *William*'s white sails over Mary's shoulder, and eventually saw the *Roger* fluttering – black against blue – through tall palm trees.

90

Truthfully, I had never seen such a welcome sight.

We left the horses in the field they had been "borrowed" from and scrambled down the rocky hillside that led to the bay. The rest of our crewmates were anxiously waiting with two rowboats ready to ferry us to the ship. It was all hands on deck now – this was the most danger we had ever faced – and every last one of us took a length of oar. We reached the *William* in no time at all and clambered up the rope ladders.

Before you could recite the Lord's Prayer, we had raised anchor, trimmed the mainsail and cast off, catching a strong north-westerly wind out of the bay. As long as we were sailing in a prevailing wind, I knew none of the flotilla I had seen moored in Nassau would catch us. The *William* was smaller, but she was faster. And we had at least a fifteen-furlong head start, even if the governor had the slightest clue where we were.

When we were sober and frightened for our lives, I decided the crew of the *William* were hard to beat. We knew how to drink. We knew how to fight. And we knew when to run away.

***

We sailed as fast and as straight as we could, until the wind dropped and the sun began to set portside. I took some private time to clean myself up in captain's quarters, sponging off the blood from my body as best I could until I could properly bathe, and soaking the rope burns on my wrists in a bucket of sea water. I dressed in a fresh shirt, tied a bandana around my head, pulled on clean trousers and boots and – at cries of "land ho!" – went out to help furl the mainsail. Men's clothes had never felt so good.

We lowered the anchor next to a group of tiny cays which Solomon, our navigator, reckoned were around five leagues off the north-eastern coast of

Andros Island. The islands were deserted as far as the eye could see – turquoise blue waters gently washed up on dazzling white shores, dotted with the occasional fat crab. Beyond the pristine beaches, thick-leafed rubber plants clung densely around palm trees, their trunks sprouting upwards and over, as if weighed down by the glut of plump green coconuts which – even from where we stood onboard – we could see burgeoning beneath their branches. From all the way up on the *William*'s forecastle deck, we could see the water surrounding the ship teemed with large green turtles and brightly coloured fish.

It felt like we had arrived in paradise.

"Somebody get me more ammo!" Jack shouted excitedly, leaning over the rail. "And bring me some bloody rum. We're feasting on turtle tonight!"

While the crew picked off the fattest turtles they could see, Mary and I went to fetch a barrel of grog from the larder and more bullets from quarters.

"Are you feeling all right?" Mary asked, as I picked up Jack's blackjack tankard from the bedstand. Its leather coating was well worn from countless nights carousing.

I turned and kissed her quickly, my arms full of supplies. "Don't fuss, Mary. I'm still breathin' and all in one piece, thanks to you. But…as it happens, I am more than a little interested…exactly how much convincin' did Jack require to agree to my rescue?"

She had the grace to look away from me and paused at length before she replied. "A knife to his throat clinched the deal," she said, her jaw tight with tension.

I had suspected as much but said nothing more, simply happy to be free, at sea, and back with Mary. "Come on, let's celebrate," I said lightly, and kissed her again.

We carried everything out to deck, where the crew were laughing and cheering, hoisting huge turtles out of the water with grappling hooks.

Together, we tossed everything we required into the rowboats – still lashed astern in the haste of our escape – and the entire crew rowed to the nearest island.

We built a huge fire on the beach from driftwood and dried palm leaves and spit-roasted one turtle after another until we had had more than our fill of the succulent, rich meat. By the time darkness fell, three barrels of booze were empty, and Jack and the crew could not string a sentence together. They lay on the sand, giggling and hiccupping. It was only a matter of time, I knew, before they fell into a deep sleep.

I squeezed Mary's knee in the darkness. "Come with me?"

We rose silently and walked along the beach, our fingers brushing against each other's, until the orange glow of the campfire was well out of sight. I took a long swig of rum from a wineskin and passed it to Mary. When I watched her mouth cover where my lips had been, I felt a sudden flood of warmth. It bloomed deep within me, swirling and shifting pleasantly, like slow-moving honey. I stepped away from her and pulled off my boots, tossing them onto the sand.

"I need to bathe," I said.

Slowly, I unbuttoned my breeches and pushed them off, kicking them to one side. Then I moved further away, stepping backwards into the warm shallow waters.

Mary grew entirely still as she watched me undress, as if she were sculpted in marble. Her eyes were intense, dark and wide – like pools of scalding hot oil in the moonlight.

My breath caught in my throat.

Mary wanted me. I had seen that look directed at me many times before and I knew it well. This time it felt different. *Mary wanted me.*

I held her gaze as boldly as I could. I took a deep breath to steady myself, and in one fluid motion pulled off my shirt. Despite the warmth of the evening, goosebumps prickled all over my bare skin.

My breath came quickly in short, shallow gasps.

I yearned for her to touch me.

Instantly, as if she had been reanimated by a sudden bolt of lightning, Mary flung off her coat and strode, fully clothed, into the sea, grabbing my face and kissing me deeply. I wasted no time unbuttoning her shirt and breeches, filling my palms with her warm, pliant breasts and cleaving my hips against hers. She felt wonderful to me. Strong and soft, powerful and gentle, all at once. I had a sudden, fleeting revelation: *no wonder men desire us so ardently*.

She moaned and swept her palms down my back, cupping my backside, dipping her fingers briefly into my centre, and lifted me so my legs wrapped around her waist. Robbed of breath, I pulled my lips from hers and latched my mouth onto her neck as she carried me further into the sea.

In that moment, it felt as though we were the only two people on that island, on the Earth. Somewhere outside of time. We were caught in the eye of a mighty squall, a swirling maelstrom of sensation.

"I belong to you now, Mary," I whispered, my voice thick with emotion. "You, and the sea."

12

We spent many happy months on the *William* after that. Mary and I did not reveal ourselves to Jack or the crew and we were able to steal moments together most days. Some nights, when the men had had too much rum and all passed out cold below deck, we even shared a bed. We would make love and talk for hours – gazing up at the stars through the windows – recounting our battles, loves, and losses, wondering at our shared similarities, our uncanny connection, and the serendipitous converging of our lives.

"I have never been so happy, Mary," I said one night in bed, tracing her palm with my fingertips. "My life began with you on this ship."

She linked our hands together, kissed me soundly on the mouth and began to sing:

Annie and me, Annie and me, born of the sea, always will be.

Annie and me of the sea.

Happy we'll be, born of the sea, Annie and me of the sea.

Then she leaned over me, reached into her coat pocket, and pulled out a thin gold necklace. A single pink pearl dangled from the chain.

I gasped. "Is that a —"

"Queen conch pearl? Yes. I found one. On *our* island, Annie."

She unclasped the necklace and carefully fastened it around my neck. She smiled at me. Kissed my mouth, my neck, the pearl, my chest. Then she moved lower.

***

That was our last night on the *William*. Early the next morning the ship came under a devastating attack from an English warship, its plentiful cannonballs blasting our hull to smithereens, shocking us from our slumber.

Mary and I tore out from our quarters, barely clothed. The ship loomed above us like a pale mountain, a vast three-masted 120-foot sloop-of-war. As it drew alongside, I saw two-score of armed sailors standing at the taffrails, ready to lower their gangways onto the *William*. The men were smartly dressed in black greatcoats with gold buttons that gleamed in the morning sun.

Mary and I looked at each other, our eyes wide with fear and an unmistakeable sense of foreboding.

"I am not going down without a fight, Annie," Mary said fiercely.

I kissed her, refusing to acknowledge that this might be the end. "I wouldn't want it any other way."

She ran her fingertips along my jaw. Then she turned and charged forwards with both her swords drawn.

"Jack!" I screamed. *"LADS!* Main deck, now!"

I stuck my head into the stairwell and hollered for them again, but there was no response. I whipped my head back towards Mary. Two gangways had already been lowered and men were beginning to make their way over. She positioned herself at the end of the first gangway and began to fight off the onslaught.

We were out of time.

I sprinted to the second ramp to defend against the other line of invaders.

Mary and I fought the men alone for as long as we could. Jack and the crew stayed below decks the whole time, most likely still drunk and scared. As it turned out, there was a good reason why Jack only took small ships.

These men were a different breed of fighter to any I had faced before. Mercenaries. Well trained and well organised, they swung their swords at me with such precision and strength that, soon, all I could do was dodge the blows.

Eventually, two of them managed to disarm and restrain me. Mary continued fighting valiantly for a while, her face showing the despair I felt, all the while screaming for the crew to come and help us. She even fired a pistol below decks in vain, such was her bitter disappointment. (Later, we found out that she had killed our boat swain. We were both aggrieved it was not Jack.)

Finally, when Mary was surrounded by men and it was all too clear we stood no chance, I pleaded with her – urging her to surrender, terrified she would be killed. In desperation, I cried out that we were both women. There was simply nothing else I could think to do to ensure her survival.

The entire crew were arrested by the warship's captain, a privateer turned pirate-hunter named Jonathan Barnet, who had been hired to pursue and detain Jack and me, and our crew, thanks to a tip-off from an informant of Governor Woodes Rogers. That informant, I later found out, was none other than a bitter and revengeful James Bonny.

Mary and I decided to lie and "plead our bellies" – pretending we were both pregnant – to delay our own trials, at least for a short time.

Before his piracy trial in Port Royal, Jack requested to see me in the cell I shared with Mary, due to my reported condition and his apparent paternity. When the gaoler brought him, I could barely hold Mary back from strangling Jack through the bars.

"Woah. Steady, woman!" Jack leant back, keeping a safe distance from Mary's clawing hands. "Well, well. Who'd'a guessed it...Mark Read, a *woman*, no less! Still canny believe that one, such a strong fighter. And, so I hear, a woman in no condition to fight me right now. Although I have been wonderin' which of my crewmen managed to sneak you a stiff one."

"You are a sorry *coward*, Jack," Mary spat, shaking with fury. "We could've taken on that warship if you had grown a pair."

"Ahh, come now. *Mary*, is it? We both know I have more than you will *ever* have. Anne can testify to that, can't you, Anne?"

Mary leapt against the bars, trying desperately to gain an extra inch to reach him with her fingernails. I placed a soothing hand on her shoulder, brushed my lips against her cheek, and walked calmly to the cell door. I knew it was no use trying to reason with Jack – he had valued bluff and charm above bravery all the time I had known him.

I stood face to face with him, knowing this would be the last time I would ever see him.

"Despite reports to the contrary, I do not carry your child," I said. I could scarcely contain my disgust at the notion. "I'm sorry to see you here, Jack. But it is richly deserved. If only you had fought like a man, you needn't be hanged like a dog. And outfought by two *women*! Ha! Soon, every soul alive will know the legendary Calico Jack was a cowardly dog when it truly counted. And a cowardly dog is *always* how you shall be remembered. Even you can't talk yourself out of it, this time."

He had no response to that. He could not even summon the courage to look me in the eye.

"Take me back to my cell," he growled at the gaoler.

That was the last time I set eyes on Jack Rackham. He was trialled and executed along with the rest of the crew the very next day. I heard later that his hanged body was put on display in a gibbet cage at Deadman's Cay outside Port Royal, to serve as a deterrent against a life of piracy.

106

Well, every dog deserves a cage.

***

Mary and I spent several weeks together in that cold, dark cell. There was no natural light and the walls were mouldy and damp, but we made the best of it for a time; talking and singing to each other. We knew that sooner or later it would be plain as day that neither of us was quick with child.

Before long, Mary began to get sick.

"Annie," Mary whispered, light and delicate as a feather against my throat.

"Yes, my love?"

I held her feverish brow to my chest and stroked my fingertips through her wet hair.

"Promise me...you'll get out. Your father...or James...will come for you. Promise me...you'll do whatever it takes...to escape."

"I'm not leaving you. I'm never leaving you."

She shifted between my legs and the scrape of her boots rang around the cell. She tipped her head just enough to look at me. In a face contorted with pain, her blue eyes were still a calm pool of strength in the darkness, as they always had been for me.

"I'll be leaving you soon enough, Annie. There's nowt we can do about that."

"No," I said, fiercely. "You'll be fine. You'll pull through and we'll both get out."

Her eyes crinkled like water boatmen's tracks. She dipped her head back onto my chest and we stayed that way for a while. Then she took a deep, rattling breath and sang our song, weakly, almost imperceptibly:

Annie and me, Annie and me, born of the sea,
always will be.
Annie and me of the sea.

After that, she was lost in her fever for three more days. No one came to help. I held her desperately close, willing her to return, waiting to hear her voice again, to feel her strength, her warmth, hoping for a miracle that never came.

13

My name, in those days, was Anne Bonny.

These days, I go by the name Annie Read.

Some days, I dream of my life as a pirate. I wake looking out to sea; sometimes in bed, sometimes tucked into my rocker with a tweed blanket, and feel that old familiar excitement still fizzing in my belly. I remember those days from long ago with a strange mixture of pride and regret.

Some days I wake with no memory of dreams at all, simply grateful for the life I have been able to live out in Charles Town, surrounded by family.

Every now and then, I dream of Mary.

These dreams bring the sweetest ache to my fragile, elderly body. When I wake in these precious moments, I try to hold on to that fleeting feeling of pleasure-pain, that sharp prick of desire, that brief, transcendent moment before the crushing grief arrives, when my body awakens remembering what my mind cannot; still suffused with the memory of her warmth, her voice, her mouth, her love.

Thank You!

Thank you so much for reading my novella. If you enjoyed it, please consider leaving an honest, fair review on your preferred site, or recommend it to some friends. It *really* helps – one short review or a good recommendation via word-of-mouth makes a massive difference to independent authors like me.

If you like my style, you can read more about me or sign up for new releases, giveaways, and other news at www.kate-castle.com. My debut full-length novel, *Girl Island*, is being published soon.

I am also on most social media platforms @katecastlebooks. Get in touch – I would be absolutely delighted to hear from you!

You can turn over a few pages here, too, for a little bit more about me and my writing.

Thank you, again.

Kate x

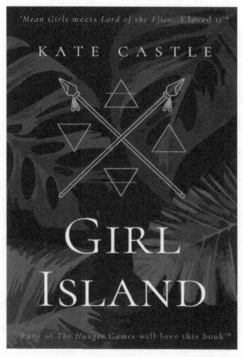

About the Author

Kate Castle has a degree in English Literature and lives with her husband and three children in Essex, England.

Kate's books fall into the New Adult and Young Adult romance and adventure categories. She is passionate about representing young queer females in mainstream literature and writes about strong, independent, fluid young women – the kind of characters she wished she could have read more about growing up.

She is a proud representative and vocal champion of bisexual fiction (affectionately coined by Kate as 'BiFi') as an up-and-coming genre and continues to write in this exciting and original domain.

Read more about Kate and sign up to her mailing list at www.kate-castle.com or on socials @katecastlebooks.

Author's Note & Acknowledgements

Although a work of fiction, *Born of the Sea* is based on the (unbelievably!) true story of trailblazing pirates Anne Bonny and Mary Read and was developed through my lifelong fascination with pirates and these two buccaneers in particular. These were two women way ahead of their time – I have always wanted to tell their story. During my research, I came across many sources which report that Anne and Mary were most likely lovers. This very real possibility, together with the inseparable duo's widely reported scandalous gender-bending, cross-dressing, fighting, looting, boozing and eventual imprisonment (and Mary's death) – in a world of men, no less – was all the inspiration I needed to write an unconventional, passionate love story between these two remarkable women. A story which, so far, seems to have been untold – at least in romance fiction. It has been a pleasure and a privilege for me to tell

Anne and Mary's tale. I hope you fall in love with them, too.

A very big thank you to my earliest supporters who loved what they read and encouraged me to finish the story and take it through to publication; especially Timmo, Miriama and Lottie. Thank you to my brilliant editors, Carrie O'Grady and Nick Taylor, for their encouragement, sage advice and total enthusiasm for Anne and Mary's story. Thanks too to my beta and ARC readers for all their feedback and reviews. Especially my Earper gang – I froggin' love you guys.

To my wonderful children: as I am always saying, never be afraid to be who you are, or to love who you love. Conformity is for wimps. *There is only one you for all eternity.* Fearlessly be yourself, and you will find your people. This story is a good reminder of that.

Finally, my deepest thanks and devotion goes to Tim for his unwavering support and love. Thank

you for understanding and loving all the parts of me.
A lesser man would have bailed years ago.

Glossary & Fun Facts

Avast: an exclamation, interjection, or command, meaning to stop or cease.

Barrelman: a sailor stationed in the crow's nest of a ship.

Cribbage: a popular card game, often played by pirates.

Furlong: an eighth of a mile, approximately 220 yards.

League: approximately 3 miles.

Pettifogger: an inferior legal practitioner, one who used dubious means to get clients.

Pleading the belly: a common law practice whereby a woman received reprieve of a death sentence until after she bore her child.

Roger: slang for the *Jolly Roger* – a black and white flag, often featuring a skull design, flown from many pirate ships.

Swiving: having sexual intercourse.

Pirates designed their own version of the Jolly Roger as a kind of individual brand. But Jack Rackham is credited as its original creator. The original Jolly Roger flag flown from Jack Rackham's ship is shown below. The pair of crossed cutlasses was said to represent Anne Bonny and Mary (Mark) Read. The skull represented Calico Jack. Our infamous trio sailed the Caribbean seas together for many months under this flag before their eventual arrest and trial in November 1720.

Pierre, the dressmaker, was a real person and was widely known among pirates as "Pierre the Pansy Pirate". His real name was Pierre Bouspet. He is reported to have owned a café, a hairdresser's and a dressmaking business and was a popular figure with pirates throughout the Caribbean.

With no women around, homosexual relationships were thought to be commonplace among pirates at sea. Indeed, *matelotage* was a kind of pirate gay marriage – a same-sex civil partnership where two men agreed to share their wealth and belongings and, if one should die, the other would benefit by inheriting their partner's property. The word "mate", used commonly on board ships, was most likely derived from the French word *"matelotage"*.

As it turns out, the Golden Age of Piracy was way ahead of its time in more ways than one!